Hi, I'm Madison
D1592281

DEDICATION

This book is dedicated to my love and my legacy
Vernon and Madison Beckford

MADISON'S 1ST DOLLAR

A Picture Book About Money

by Ebony Beckford

MADISON'S 1ST DOLLAR

Written by Ebony Beckford

Madison just got her first dollar

This will give her major buying power
Toys
Savings
POW!
BOOM!
Candy
BAM!
Donations

What do you think she should do with it?

TOYS
TOYS

Should she ask her mommy to take her to the store?

Save
Give
Spend

Or save her dollar until she gets more?

Candy
shop

Should she spend a little now?

And save the rest for later?

Or should she donate it all to help out a neighbor?

LEMONADE
Invest

Should she put away 25 cents to invest?

For
Charity

Or should she give away 25 cents
because she feels so blessed?

Should she spend 50 cents to
buy a friend a surprise?

Maddie' Savings Plan:
Spend - 50 cents
Save - 25 cents
Give - 25 cents

Or create a savings plan
because that would be wise?

THE UNITED STATES OF AMERICA
B77578065G
B77578065G
ONE DOLLAR

Whatever Madison decides to
do, I'm sure it will be fun
and responsible too!

Tell us how you would spend YOUR dollar!

(Write your answer in the bubble below)

Color and cut out the money below

Color and cut out the money below

Color and cut out the money below

Color and cut out the money below

Color and cut out the money below

Color and cut out the money below

Made in the USA
Monee, IL
03 December 2020

50783355R00026